ABOUT THE AUTHOR

Since 2000, David Mason has worked in schools all over the country and abroad, teaching children how to be terribly dramatic and write stories and poems. He has written 25 books. He has six wonderful children and a lovely wife.

ABOUT THE ILLUSTRATOR

This is the sixth book with illustrations by Helen Mason, David's wife. She loves drawing lots of silly pictures with her digital pen and paint. She also writes blogs about all sorts of things to do with books, poetry and their family's exciting adventures

www.guidetoselfpublishinguk.blogspot.co.uk
www.homeeducationwithcurriculum.blogspot.co.uk

There's even a brand new blog for Mr Smile:
www.mrsmileshappyblog.blogspot.co.uk

Take a look at David Mason's website for more information on his work and books:
www.InspiretoWrite.co.uk

Publishing Information

"Mr Smile Investigates...Ten Ways to Happiness" © David J. Mason
2014
All rights reserved
Published by: North Street Publishing
Publishing address: North Street Publishing
14 Ribblesdale Avenue, Congleton, Cheshire CW12 2BS
Telephone: 01260 291898   www.InspireToWrite.co.uk
Email: Enquiries@InspireToWrite.co.uk

Illustrations by Helen J. E. Mason © 2014

Print ISBN 978-0-9569287-5-7

Printed by Orbital Print Services Ltd
Staplehurst Road, Sittingbourne, Kent ME10 2NH
www.orbitalprint.co.uk

Table of Contents

Dedication

Eternal thanks to my wonderful friend Lynn Ferguson whose big smile and positive attitude to life will remain with me, forever.

HM

"That's happiness for you. As long as you are spreading happiness wherever you go, you will enjoy a wonderful life. Everything else follows. Nothing else matters as much as true happiness"

Mr Smile

Or, as Mr Smile could have said, "Perfect love drives out fear" 1 John 4:18

DM

4

Chapter One - Mr Smile's World

Mr Smile didn't live in the real world, or so people said. That didn't bother Mr Smile; he liked his other world. Some people thought this other world was impossible and made up and, well, quite frankly really far-fetched. That didn't bother Mr Smile either. He had always lived there and had no plans to leave.

In fact, if the truth be told (and Mr Smile was a very honest fellow) he had not even heard of the real world or the people that lived there and what they had to say or what they thought. He was happy here and that was that.

Mr Smile had been born with a smile upon his face and it had stayed there ever since. It was indeed a grand smile. It stretched almost, but not quite, from ear to ear. It was such a big part of his face. Why, it *was* his face!

'That's why I am called Mr Smile,' he said to himself as he cleaned his flashing white teeth after breakfast each morning. 'My friends began by calling me Mr Smile and I suppose the name just stuck – like my smile!'

From time to time, Mr Smile wondered at the wonder of his smile. Why did it never disappear? Why was it always, always so strong and healthy?

One afternoon, sitting in his cosy cottage, Mr Smile puzzled over these questions. After a few minutes he gave up puzzling and concluded that some things were meant to be. Besides, what was the point in worrying himself about such matters when he could be relaxing, eating toast with creamy butter?

He liked toast. No, he *adored* toast, every single crumb of it. Every morning, he would awake excited at the thought of his toast and that feeling of excitement would grow and grow.

He loved the trip to the baker's each day. The walk down the winding lane was an absolute delight – there was so much to see and hear, including his nicely empty, rumbling tummy!

Then there was the smell of the new-baked bread in the baker's. It made Mr Smile wonder where his loaf had come from: It all began in Winter when the seed would be sown but would lay there for the most part, sleeping under the snow. In Spring, the green shoots would appear and the wheat would start to grow. By Summer the tall crop would be waving in the warm breeze. Autumn and the ripe golden heads would be ready for harvest. Then the grains would be milled into flour and the baker would mix the dough and bake Mr Smile's loaf. Wow! He must never take his treasured loaf for granted.

The baker always gave him a great big smile to match his own and Mr Smile would leave for home, holding tight his prize loaf. The return journey was equally exciting. There was the anticipation of that first bite, that fresh bread taste and the satisfaction of a full tummy afterwards.

'So,' thought Mr Smile, as he began to munch on his afternoon toast treat, 'there's so much more to this toast than just eating it. It makes me happy in so many ways.'

Mr Smile sat up straight. "That's it," he pronounced to no one but himself, "I have found the secret of my smile and so the happiness that

keeps me smiling: it is...toast!" And with that, he
smiled.

Chapter Two - Another World

Mr Smile made a habit of an afternoon nap. All he needed was fifteen magical minutes. He would always wake refreshed to enjoy the rest of the day.

This afternoon was no exception. Mr Smile yawned his yawn that announced the beginning of his nap and carried it on with, of course, a smile upon his face.

Mr Smile quickly fell into a very, very deep sleep – much deeper than the deepest sleep he had ever slept. It was definitely all the wondering about his smile, it had simply worn him out.

He dreamed of another world, the *real world*, a deep dark voice kept reminding him. It wasn't a very nice place; it was a sad, unfriendly and frightening place.

In his dream, Mr Smile woke up as usual in his cottage. He washed and cleaned his teeth before setting off for his morning walk to the baker's. He let himself out of his front door as usual.

He found himself walking on a quite different lane from his lane. He didn't recognise the sights or sounds as he journeyed. Without warning, a mist descended. The air turned cold. He stood still as a statue. He was lonely, lost. A terrible silence settled all about him.

(At this point, Mr Smile tried very hard to wake himself up and escape from his dream but his brain wouldn't let him.)

Mr Smile shivered. Worse was to come. The mist departed as quickly as it had arrived. The heavens were revealed, filled with masses of huge grey and black clouds, swirling about the sky.

A strong wind. A gale. A hurricane (or so it seemed) knocked Mr Smile off his feet. Rain hammered down from above. Lightning leapt from side to side, up and down. Thunder boomed.

Mr Smile tried to pick himself out of the mud but the monstrous weather held him in its clutches. Mr Smile held out a shaking hand. Surely someone would help him? Surely there was someone nearby who would take pity on a stranger in need?

No. Figures appeared on the scene but they simply stood and watched Mr Smile struggle. That was bad enough but it was their faces that really worried him. Every face, old or young, was thoroughly miserable. Every one of them wore a heavy frown. Their eyes were dark and empty. Their mouths were straight and sad. There was not a smile to be seen on any of those faces.

Mr Smile lowered his head. He thought he'd rather look at the mud than all the misery.

All at once, fingers reached out from somewhere. Mr Smile saw them from the corner of his eye. He looked up. His eyes were met by another pair peering down at him: a sad pair of grey eyes belonging to a small boy. The boy's clothes were grey, his skin was grey. His voice was weak and whining.

"Can you help us, sir? Please, please. We're desperate. Look at me, sir. Look at everyone around you. I want us to learn to smile – like you. You can show us how to. You must have the secret. You're our only hope."

The small boy clasped his hands together.

"I beg of you. Please, please. Don't leave us to our misery."

Mr Smile tried to say something but the words wouldn't come out. Still the pitiful image hovered above him. He couldn't bear it any longer. He must pick himself up out of the mud...

Suddenly Mr Smile woke and found himself trying to push himself out of his comfy chair. He breathed a sigh and settled back down into his favourite seat. So, it was all a silly dream. Nothing more. Just something he'd made up inside his own head – or was it?

It was not silly! It was a **terrible** dream! It was the sort of dream that would take the smile off anyone's face – except Mr Smile – but even he felt the corners of his mouth twitching.

Was it a dream? Yes, well it was and it wasn't. Dreams are not supposed to be real. This felt very real. So real that he couldn't just forget about this other world. Those people needed him. The boy had said it all. He was sure the other world existed, but where? And what about the boy, did he really exist?

He couldn't answer these questions all by himself. No, that's what friends were for. There was a certain someone who could help him.

Mr Smile took a good long look at his old friend the clock that sat ever so comfortably upon his mantelpiece and seemed to smile back at him.

"Good, very good. Not too late then."

He rushed out on to the lane, leaving the door swinging upon its hinges. Not to worry, Mr Smile's neighbours were too happy to be burgling. In fact they were quite the opposite, always trying to give things away but Mr Smile didn't need anything – all he really needed was his smile.

He didn't really need hot cross buns for tea but then he did need an excuse to visit the baker and ask his advice. You couldn't ask a baker for advice unless you were prepared to buy a few of his buns. No, that was only polite.

Mr Smile pushed open the bakery door, breathing deeply to make the most of the marvellous aroma of freshly baked bread and cakes.

"Aaaaah!," he exhaled and, in the same breath, ordered the buns.

He looked around the shop – no other customers, good!

"Mr Baker, I need your help. You haven't by any chance heard of another world, have you? I think they may call it the *real* world."

Mr Baker beamed. "I have, as a matter of fact. One or two of my customers say they know of someone who has been there but I've never met them. I've heard a little bit about it, though."

"I see," nodded Mr Smile.

"Yes," continued the baker, not smiling so much now and seeming to speak to himself, "it's not a place most people would bother visiting. It's not a place I would ever visit."

"Why? Why wouldn't you visit?"

"Well, it sounds an awfully long journey up and down mountains, through forests, over rivers, across grasslands, on and on and on. Then, when you finally arrive, the place is miserable."

"That doesn't sound so good."

"No, but perhaps I am being a little too gloomy. There's always the castle to look forward to."

"The castle?" Mr Smile liked the sound of a castle.

"Yes, the castle marks the boundary between here and there. One of our lot built it. It's supposed to be the final reminder of our beautiful world before it all turns rather dark and depressing crossing into theirs."

14

The baker paused a moment or two before his face brightened considerably. "You'd be alright though! Fit and healthy chap like yourself and what with that smile of yours, you'd warm the cockles of anyone's heart. Yes, come to think of it, you of all people could pay them a visit. You're a bit of a free spirit, aren't you? You only have your clock to look after; I've a bakery and hungry customers."

The baker leaned closer. "Are you by any chance thinking of going?"

"Yes, as a matter of fact I am. I am on a sort of, well – a mission."

"A mission?"

"Yes, well perhaps, but really more of an adventure with a little bit of a mission. In fact maybe the mission is the adventure. Anyway," said Mr Smile, hurrying on and not wanting to answer any more questions, "like you say, I haven't exactly anything to lose, have I?"

"No, except your smile!" the baker laughed. "No, seriously, we would miss you around here. You really do brighten up this place."

"Well, who knows? I am not absolutely sure about the adventure – but if I did go, I hope to return here even happier than when I left."

"Is that possible?"

"I believe it is," said Mr Smile, grinning, and quietly closing the bakery door behind him.

So that was that. Now he knew he must go. He had found out all that he needed to know. Thank goodness for his friend the baker!

On his way back home, he began to think about his trip. The days were lengthening now. The sun was setting later in the evening and rising earlier in the morning. It must be Spring. Spring was a splendid season for travel; he would leave the next morning. Before that, he would eat a proper sportsman's tea – the hot cross buns – and go to bed early, like all good athletes.

That evening Mr Smile spent planning. He would definitely travel alone. Anyway, he doubted whether anyone would want to come with him. They probably wouldn't understand why he was going on his adventure. Yes, he would miss the jolly baker and his other friends but he would think

of them all the time he was away and share his adventures with them on his return.

He would have with him his very important notebooks and pens, the best that money could buy. He would use these to record all his thoughts and all his observations as he journeyed through the mountains, the forests and the grasslands. Then, after he had reached the castle and crossed into the other world, he could begin writing all about the people from the other world.

Mr Smile had another idea. He almost exploded when it came to him. "I know!" he announced, "I'll write a book!" He felt all shivery and terribly creative. "I want to help those people so I will write a book for them, telling them the secrets of happiness. Then, whenever they feel miserable, they can read a chapter or two and remind themselves of how to make themselves happy.

"And," said Mr Smile, very loudly, as he almost burst with bubbles of ideas, "I'll make a copy to bring home with me in case anyone in my world needs a little help. Or maybe they will read it just because it's interesting. And of course it will be interesting because it is all about life and how to be happy."

Mr Smile's thoughts turned to his dream and the boy in his dream, the one who begged him for help. That boy certainly needed the book. Was the boy a real boy? If so, would he meet him? Mr

Smile dared to hope so. There was only one way to find out.

Mr Smile couldn't sleep; his head was full of plans, notebooks and pens. As soon as the waking sun crept into his room, he bounced from his bed. He checked himself in the mirror...and smiled.

He didn't like goodbyes. All the fuss and bother about leaving. And, if he was honest, all the sadness. No, he would slip away quietly. The baker would know where he'd gone and that he'd definitely return.

He patted his faithful clock and smoothed the soft seat of his favourite chair. Too excited to eat, Mr Smile left in a flash, not forgetting to leave the door open behind him.

Chapter Three – The Journey begins

Mr Smile whistled while he walked. As he journeyed over the lowlands, he kept his eye on the lonely mountains rising in the distance. His target spurred him on.

"You've a visitor coming to see you. I am sure we will enjoy each other's company," he told them.

Crossing these lowlands was like strolling around his village. Yes, it was a considerable distance but the walking wasn't difficult.

The mountains, however, presented a very different challenge. Mr Smile had to huff and puff his way up steep and narrow paths. Every so often he would stop to admire the view and to look back to where he had come from.

After a long struggle he would at last reach a peak. Sitting up there he felt he could almost touch the sky. The cooler air cleared his head. Mr Smile thought thoughts he thought were impossible to think!

Words bounced about his brain. Ideas came to him in flashes, one after another. Like one of the ancient gods, he sat up on the highest peak. He took out his notebook and pen. He eased open the perfect, thick cover. He picked up his favourite pen and...paused...and...continued to pause. Right now the pen in his hand felt awkward.

Supposing he just wasn't a writer? There would be no book. His adventure would be just an adventure. He wouldn't be able to help anyone. Yet he knew his travels would give him the words – eventually. They were lurking there in a bright part of his mind and they would show themselves when they were good and ready. Mr Smile was learning quickly.

'I must keep trying and learn to be patient,' he whispered to himself.

Patience was what Mr Smile needed as he made his difficult descent from the mountain tops to the valley below. Once down in the valley he would have to climb again and then drop down into the next valley. Up and down, on and on he went.

Mr Smile was very determined. 'You never get anywhere without making an effort,' he reminded himself.

At long last he climbed up the last of the peaks and climbed down into the valley where the forest began.

'No more mountains,' he said to himself with a sigh of relief. ' But, on second thoughts, I've really enjoyed your company – and I will return, you wait and see.'

Looking back, he was sure he saw the mountains smiling down upon him.

On the edge of the forest, the trees were evenly spaced so that Mr Smile could move easily between them. The sun's rays reached into the wide, light spaces where he strolled, gazing up into the wondrous green canopy.

As he moved towards the middle of the forest, so the bigger trees grew much closer together. There were smaller trees stretching upwards to reach daylight. It was shady here and in some places, almost dark. Here where the going became tougher, Mr Smile had to smash, crash and bash his way through the tangled undergrowth. He carried a heavy stick with him at all times.

Smashing, crashing and bashing made his arms ache a great deal so he was glad when the thorny shrubs and scrub gave way to the odd clear passage where he could tread lightly on the soft, peaty soil carpet beneath his tired feet.

The forest though, was a great place to find great food. Fruits of all shapes and sizes hung from trees and bushes, ripe for plucking. Juicy berries presented themselves for his picking. Mr Smile wasn't a fussy eater; he licked his lips, enjoying every mouthful. The fresh food tasted wonderful and certainly put a spring in Mr Smile's step.

However, nothing it seemed, was ever straight-forward. There were wide rivers running through the forest. Now, Mr Smile didn't carry a compass. He must try to keep going in as straight a line as possible, with the sun behind him.

Mr Smile stood on the banks of the first river, one of many he must conquer. He imagined what was under the water...more water! There was more under that and scaly crocodiles with gaping jaws. There were huge shoals of poisonous black fish. There were pincers to grab, weed to strangle...!

He shivered and took a step back from the black. For the first time in his life, he felt a frown forming. What must he do? Think of something else? Don't concentrate on the darkness, look towards the light! Yes, yes! Feel the warmth of the sun on your skin.

He made himself as big as possible, laying down on the bank and stretching arms, legs, hands, fingers, feet and toes. He took his notepad and pen. To his delight, he found the words he was looking for.

Sun

Sun has a smile
A golden charm
Sun has the touch
That keeps me warm
Sun has an air
Of blissful calm
Sun has the taste
Of syrup balm.

Sun has the arms
As long as you like

Sun has the finger
Tips to give life
Sun has the face
To light up the sky
Sun has the legs
To stand straight all day.

Sun has the fame
A glittering star
Sun has the gas
Sun has the power
Sun has the colour
To make the heavens glow
Sun is the spirit
Worshipped from below.

He was a writer after all! Well now, by thinking and writing about his friend the sun, he felt so much better. Simple! He stood up and watched, as indeed the sun smiled down on him and winked.

He turned once more to the river. This time he saw the sun's rays reflecting on the water. Diamonds danced. There was hope and joy here now.

Mr Smile swam, keeping his head high and looking to the layer of water all about him and the sun above him. He arrived wet but safe and, sitting on the other side, felt his heart grow that little bit stronger from the exercise.

Mr Smile walked and swam and walked and swam through the depths of the forest. He crossed five rivers in all. He smashed and bashed a path in between. He never once thought about giving up and going back.

Eventually he reached the far edge of the forest. There was space to rest here. He sat down in the shade of a magnificent tree. In the silence, he looked, listened and thought. He pictured the fruit he had eaten, all the birds, bugs and bigger animals that lived in the trees and the protection the tree proffered to all living things. Another story or perhaps a poem! He could say a great big thank you to the tree for all those things he hadn't noticed before this wondrous journey began. Why yes! Once more, the words poured from his pen.

Tree

Our famous forest
A place of great charm
But do spare a thought
For the tree and his arms

Those branches outstretched
To hold up the sky
No wonder they drop off
From time to time

And what of his roots
With all of that standing?

No wonder his bunions
And nodules are swelling

His back bent over
Arched with the effort
His trunk invaded
By burrowing insects

In later years
He knows no pension
Still he endeavours
To stand to attention

Our good old soldier
The forest dweller
Here's three cheers
For a jolly brave fella!

After all that smashing, crashing and bashing, all that swimming and now the writing, you might just think that Mr Smile was very tired. Perhaps he was exhausted and could not carry on, unable to put one foot in front of the other. Not a chance!

You see, at night-time Mr Smile was sleeping like a baby so he woke each morning with all the energy in the world. Why did he sleep so well?

Well, during the day, the sun shone brilliantly in an endless blue sky. This left only the night time for the rain to fall and water the world. The clouds would sneak into the sky as soon as the sun had given up and gone to bed.

The rain would pitter-patter down upon hard rocks, soft soils and glassy rivers. It would drip-drop from the leaves of the trees, collect in crystal pools and flow on and on in running rivulets. It conjured up the rhythm of sleep and Mr Smile, like the rest of us, fell under its spell.

'I've never felt so wonderfully calm,' Mr Smile reflected. 'It's the life all around me that rocks me to sleep. As I travel, I must always remember to come back to visit Nature again and again. In the company of Nature, I can find my rest.'

Leaving the forest, Mr Smile found himself in the great grasslands of this world. Full of energy he would skip, not walk, on his way. The lush emerald green grass seemed to stretch on and on forever. It was tall, reaching right up to Mr Smile's knees.

After a whole day skipping, he had to slow down a little and walk. For the first time since leaving home, he began to tire a little. He was hungry and thirsty too, he hadn't eaten since his days in the forest.

"What should a weary, hungry traveller do to help himself on his way?" Mr Smile asked.

He knew the answer. Singing always lifted his spirits. Right now it was more important than ever to sing and keep on singing as he had never done before. He sang songs about all sorts of things – all of them happy. Each had its own rhythm.

After a few hours of non-stop singing, he lay down on a soft grassy bed and made up a poem in his head.

I love the kind of Music

I love the kind of music
That makes you want to dance
Puts a rhythm in your bottom
Like ants inside your pants

I love the kind of music
That makes your whole self sway
And brings out all the sunshine
And blows the clouds away.

I love the kind of music
That plays upon your heart
Puts the smile upon your face
Or makes the teardrops start.

I love the kind of music
That takes you to the beat
That makes you click your fingers
And makes you tap your feet.

I love the kind of music
That brings you to the ground
Or makes you climb all over
That mighty wall of sound.

I love the kind of music
That makes your eyes pop out
Puts the goosebumps on your skin
And makes you sing and shout.

I love the kind of music
That's mine and just for me
I hear just what I want to hear
And see what I can see.

He wrote it down. He slept soundly.

The next morning, after a little more skipping, he spied the castle in the distance. His heart leapt with joy.

Chapter Four – The Castle

By the afternoon he had arrived. The great castle door was open but there was no one about. Mr Smile stood at the castle's entrance. He peered in – still no sign of life. He decided to creep on a couple of paces – but no further – into the main hall. He didn't want to get into trouble for trespassing.

Across the hallway and to the sides, were long corridors of magnificent polished stone and ancient timber ceilings. Above him was a great gallery where minstrels might play their music and above that a turret roof.

In front of him stood a long, long dark table of the finest wood. The table was set for a feast; food was piled up on several plates. There were two chairs, one at either end of the table.

Footsteps! Someone was approaching...slow footsteps and a tip-tapping noise.

Suddenly, Mr Smile's thoughts were clouded with doubt. He had never really considered who might live in the castle. Suppose they weren't friendly? Suppose they were very **un**friendly? Perhaps he should have knocked – silly, no one would have heard. He thought about turning and running. It was too late.

32

Mr Smile needn't have worried. The old man emerged from the dark corridor opposite wearing a smile. He held out both arms.

"Welcome," he cried in a crackly voice. "Welcome to my humble home."

Mr Smile's heart gave a great sigh of relief. He took a few steps forward towards his host and stood alongside the table.

"Why, it's beautiful," Mr Smile pronounced, "and thank you for your kind welcome. I did not want to intrude but…."

"Yes, yes," interrupted the old man as he shook Mr Smile's hand with both of his. "Don't worry, don't worry. So glad to have you here. It is I who should be thanking you for coming. Now, tell me why you're here. Tell me all about yourself. Come on! Oh…and what's your name?"

"I'm Mr Smile."

"I can see why they call you that!" the old man replied with a hearty guffaw. Mr Smile proceeded to tell the old man about the dream and his mission to save the people of the other world.

The old man was very excited and listened very carefully, nodding and shaking his head as he did so.

"And have you started the book yet?" he asked Mr Smile.

"Well, not exactly but I have written down some ideas – things I've learnt on my journey so far."

"I see – very interesting."

"And I've written poems, too."

"Well, well! Please let me read them."

The old man read and re-read Mr Smile's writings.

"These words are inspired! I'm only an old man but, do you know, I think you could be on to something here."

"Do you think so?" Mr Smile was delighted.

"I know so! Now, please, after all this excitement, I really must sit down."

The old man lowered himself into his seat, carefully.

"Would you do me a favour and pull the chair at the other end of the table close to this one? I'm not used to entertaining, you see."

The old man's smile faded.

"You're alone here?"

"Yes. Sit down and I'll tell you all about it. By the way, I'm Arthur. You know, like the knight in his castle with his round table – only I have an oblong one. Anyway, I'm pleased to meet you."

The two of them shook hands again. Mr Smile moved the other chair and sat down, eager to listen and understand. Arthur stared down at the table and began to speak, slowly and softly.

"For many years, generations of my family lived here in this splendid castle. It was, it still is, our home built by our ancestors. They were not interested in war, they simply liked the look of fairy tale castles and thought they'd build one. It was big enough to accommodate brothers and sisters, aunts and uncles, nephews and nieces and so on."

Arthur lifted his head and looked at Mr Smile.

"You should have seen the place then. You'd have loved it. It was full of love and fun."

Arthur paused, dreaming.

"Now they've all gone and, sadly, I never had any children of my own. Some died here: my own wife, my parents and their parents. Others left and never came back."

"Left? Why did they leave?"

"Because of the people from the other world, our nearest neighbours. They were so miserable – they still are. My family couldn't stand them any more. They moved away, further into this land, travelling the way from which you have just come. I can't blame them; they left to live with happy people. It happens, you know, when you are faced with the sad and miserable, you begin to lose your own smile. They wanted to be surrounded by smiles."

"I see what you mean," Mr Smile agreed, nodding and thinking of the cheery baker and all his happy neighbours.

Arthur's voice lifted. The gloomy tone was gone.

"I saw you coming from far off. Let's face it, I couldn't miss you amongst all the grass. I knew you'd be hungry and thirsty. There's not a lot to eat and drink out there. So, to celebrate your arrival, I went shopping in the other world. I visit there as little as possible nowadays. Once a year is enough. I store the food, cans and packets – I don't eat a lot."

Mr Smile saw how thin Arthur was; he looked like he could do with some proper fresh food... and hot buttered toast. Mr Smile ate heartily whilst Arthur picked at a few pieces of fruit.

"Good to see you've such an appetite. I like to see someone really enjoying themselves," said Arthur, nodding dreamily.

All at once, Arthur sat up, excited. "I must say, your smile is doing me the world of good. You really are a proper tonic, aren't you?"

"Am I?" asked Mr Smile, blushing a little.

"You certainly are!" Arthur leaned forward in his seat. "Listen, I do hope you can help those people. I do so want you to succeed but I must let you know, your task is a very, very difficult one. They have so many problems. They are doing everything wrong. That's why they are so sad. They need to know the right way to live. Your writings, your book will help them. Let's hope that is enough. You, of all people, with your smile and happy heart, should be able to teach them. And you, of all people, will not lose that smile, no matter how sad the world around you."

"Do you know, that's exactly what I think," said Mr Smile. "When you're helping people, you find extra happiness yourself. It will make me and my smile even stronger." He paused. "But what about you, Arthur? You must be lonely. Will you stay here in the castle?"

"I'm not going anywhere; I'm too old. I've lived here all my life. I couldn't settle anywhere else, this is my home."

"But what about your happiness?"

"Oh, I am not too sad. I might be a little happier but then we can't have everything we wish for, can we? Besides, I have all my happy memories."

Suddenly, Mr Smile felt the excitement rising.

"So, you do wish for a little happiness? What if I could help make that wish come true? Suppose your neighbours in the other world find happiness and pass it on to you? Suppose some of your family find out and come back here to live with you and then more of your family follow suit? Why, this castle would be like a kingdom of true...."

Arthur laughed out loud for the first time in a long while. "Stop, stop! Please, Mr Smile! That would take a miracle! It's more than I would dare ever hope for."

"Well, dare to hope, Arthur! Miracles will happen; you wait and see. Right now, if you don't mind, I'm rather keen to get on with the job. Arthur, thank you for putting on such a fine feast. Thank you for your encouragement – you, too, are a proper tonic!"

Mr Smile stood up and held out his hand for Arthur. Arthur leaned on his stick and rose to the occasion.

"I don't like good-byes." Mr Smile kept a firm grip on Arthur's hand. "I'll make you a promise – I will return. I will call again around Christmas time when I have finished my work."

"I shall be waiting for you."

"Good. And I hope to bring you the best Christmas present ever." Mr Smile winked.

Arthur winked back. "I can't wait to receive it."

"Well then," said Mr Smile, letting go of Arthur's hand, "I'd better get on with it. Which way to the other world, Arthur?"

"Simple, straight down that corridor, door at the end into a courtyard, gate straight in front of you, straight on again to the drawbridge."

"Drawbridge?"

"Yes, well actually it's just a bridge. No one ever bothered to take it up like they do in a proper castle. The neighbours are peaceful. No one wants to invade but a castle isn't a castle without a drawbridge, is it?"

"No, I suppose you're right."

"If you're keen on a little exercise, you could always forget the drawbridge and swim across the moat."

"Oh no," chuckled Mr Smile, "I've swum across enough rivers recently. I think I'd prefer the easy route – just this once."

There was an awkward silence. It was time to go. Mr Smile hesitated. Arthur tried hard not to show his sadness at their parting; his eyes were watery.

"I'll miss you, Mr Smile. Good luck."

Mr Smile felt a lump in his throat. "I'll miss you too, Arthur. Remember though, I'll be back before you know it. Remember, too, miracles can happen."

Arthur nodded. Again the silence. Finally Mr Smile smiled, turned and headed off across the hallway towards the corridor and the waiting bridge. He didn't look back. He couldn't look back. Minutes later, he crossed into the other world.

It had been a wonderful adventure so far; he had learnt so many important lessons yet there remained many still to be learned. Mr Smile didn't realise it but this other world would teach him all he needed to know.

Chapter Five – Invisible

After crossing over the drawbridge, Mr Smile would travel far and wide. He would spend nine months travelling. During that period, nobody would actually see or hear Mr Smile, except on the very last day of his stay in this world. Mr Smile was invisible. In this world, people could not see him even if his smile was standing right in front of them. They were so miserable that for them, happiness did not exist and so, Mr Smile did not exist.

Still, that would not stop him from smiling. He would have to smile. He couldn't help it. The happiness of helping others would bring the smile to his face. More importantly, he had been born Mr Smile and would remain so – all his life long.

Yes, he thought he might feel lonely from time to time but that didn't matter. It would allow him to concentrate on his work. Besides, he quite enjoyed his own company.

There was indeed a great advantage to being invisible. He could go about his daily business without worrying. No one could tell an invisible man that he didn't belong in such and such a place. He could see and hear anything he wished to see and hear.

So, Mr Smile was about to become a hidden reporter. This would allow him to discover the truth about the world and tell it to the world...

Chapter Six – March

The sun did shine, from time to time, in this world. On the first day of Spring, the great golden emperor of the sky stretched to fill the deep blue heavens. He reached out to greet all around him.

The mountains were his closest friends on the earth. They had spent the Winter shivering under a cover of pure white snow. Whilst they shivered, they slept. Now, under the warm stroking fingers of the sun, they awoke.

The snow was deep. It was hard work for the mountains to cast off their heavy blankets. In fact, it was tempting not to bother at all and to lie there all Spring and Summer.

However, there was work to do. The mountains must flex their muscles and get on with it. The sun's energy would help them to exercise.

They let go great yawns and avalanches fell from the tops to the valleys. Snow turned to water that stood still for a while before running down the mountainside. It rested, collected in lakes then ran again, racing against other little rivers. They all met at the waterfall and dived from the heights to the pools below, swirling and twirling. Mr Smile watched in wonder as the waters cascaded to the lowlands. The mighty mountains meant business.

In the forests, the trees too were beginning to come to life. If you wanted to do well you had to get to the light and that meant growing up. A tree could never take a rest. Those that did would soon die.

As one oak said to the other, "If you're lucky enough to make it out of the acorn, then don't waste your chance. No use hanging around as a little sapling all your life. You've go to go for it. You have to stretch for the sky."

So the Spring race was on. The buds opened and the leaves unfurled before the majestic sun. As they bathed in the light, the leaves made food for the trees. With the food the trees could grow.

"It's hard work but it's worth it," said the biggest oak tree in the forest. "I've been following this Spring exercise programme for the last six hundred years. I tell the younger ones if I can do it at my age then surely they can have a go. There's too much complaining nowadays, if you ask me. You just have to make the effort. Remember, as you are exercising, eventually you'll make it to the top of the trees. You have to keep your eye on the goal."

Across the forest, all the trees were limbering up for the season's growth. They stretched leg roots, branch arms and trunk bodies. If you had catkins, you shook them. If you kept your leaves on all Winter, you waved them.

"Go with the flow, let the food and drink channel through your body," cried the great oak as he led the work out. "Breathe in, breathe out," he encouraged the others. "The humans need their oxygen. Come on, step it up there!"

"Phew, this is wearing me out just thinking about it," said Mr Smile to himself. "And there was me thinking trees just stood still. Well, I never! Come to think of it, you do have to be fairly fit to stand there all day. You're like a soldier on parade, there's no rest. Imagine the effort!"

Beneath the trees bloomed the Spring flowers. The prettiest primrose amongst them had some sound advice for the others. "If you can't be bothered to stretch and exercise in the first few days of sun then, quite frankly, you'll be too late. If you sleep in, your flowers will end up pale and tatty. Your perfume will be weak and you will not attract any insects. Then you won't produce any seeds. You mark my words: only a fit flower is fit for life."

The other flowers listened and, Mr Smile noted, the forest floor was transformed from a rather dull brownish-green to an exquisite carpet of yellows, blues, whites and creams.

"I don't know where you plants get all your energy from," said Mr Smile.

"From the sun, of course," whispered the giggling flowers behind Mr Smile's back.

Mr Smile found his way to the wide, wide river. It was deep and the water was flowing quickly. In these lowlands, the river was an old man by now. He did not have the energy of the springs and streams who had so much fun tumbling down from the mountains. He wanted to take it easy now, plodding along with his walking stick in hand.

Not a chance! The melting snow had filled his channel to the brim.

"I don't like it," said the river. "I'd rather stumble on slowly but I can't. I have to almost race instead...at my age! If I didn't race, the water wouldn't reach the sea in time. My channel would fill up and overflow and then I'd flood all the fields about me. They'd be laying in deep water all Summer. Nothing could grow and the animals couldn't graze. No, even at my age, I have to be able to move fast. Let's face it, I've been training for millions of years."

"That's it," said Mr Smile, watching the river rushing on by. "I want to be just like the river. Even when I'm very old I still want to be able to move quickly when I need to. I'll need to exercise all my life to make sure that's the case."

He stood on the riverbank gazing at the magnificent countryside all about him. He didn't want to leave – but he surely had to. There were visits to be made to the villages, towns and cities where people lived. He must live amongst them to understand their ways.

'I wonder,' said Mr Smile to himself, 'if **they** are all fitness fanatics, as well.'

Mr Smile was in for a shock.

Mr Smile did not like the big town or city or whatever it was you might choose to call it. It was crowded, noisy and busy. However, he would have to get used to it. He had a job to do and he must do it properly.

Luckily, the rain of the last few days ceased and the sun met Mr Smile on his arrival there.

It was early morning. Mr Smile thought he might watch as the children made their way to school. What a wonderful day for a walk, even if there wasn't a great deal of countryside to see. A chance to breathe the air and get those legs working before you had to sit down at your desk and learn, an opportunity to swap stories with your friends.

However, there were no pedestrians on the pavements. Not a single child set foot upon them. The roads, on the other hand, were full to overflowing. In fact, some of the cars were using the pavement to try to dodge the queues of traffic. It was no use. Nothing was moving. The road to school resembled one big car park.

Traffic lights turned from red to green. Occasionally a vehicle would edge forward a little, but only a little, before the system jammed up again as cars joined the main flow from every direction.

The drivers sat glumly, their faces fixed on the bumper in front of. From time to time, a horn would sound – someone was angry. Other horns would follow, and yet more as drivers suddenly lost patience.

After a mad few seconds, this terrible racket would cease. The car engines would continue their rumbling, hissing, spitting and spluttering, the air thick with exhaust fumes.

The children were locked inside the cars. They sat as statues. Their mouths did not move. They didn't speak. Their glazed expression seemed to suggest they didn't see. To keep themselves alive, they breathed in the filtered air circulating inside their parents' taxis.

"Oh well," said Mr Smile, "let's hope for better things at school. Things will be different, when the children step into their school playground. They'll be able to stretch those legs and enjoy a good run around. They'll certainly need it after that journey to school."

He walked about the playground. He was very surprised and disappointed with what he saw. Nearly all the children stood around in large groups. A few talked to each other. Most didn't. None of them moved.

There was the odd child on the edge of the group clutching a tennis ball or a skipping rope, or one rolling a football to and fro beneath their foot. They were asking others to play with them but nobody wanted to.

Someone suggested a game of chase. Everyone else groaned and shook their heads.

"A running race?" another proposed.

"You must be joking!" came the reply.

The bell sounded and the children trudged into school, heads down. Their faces were grim. They didn't look as though they were about to enjoy their learning.

At playtime it was the same again, then again at lunchtime. The children could move their mouths to chew on snacks, sandwiches or school lunches, but that was it.

Mr Smile couldn't help himself. He yawned again and again. It made him feel tired, just watching them. Was there any life in this town?

He would visit the swimming pool. He had developed quite an interest in swimming since his adventures in the rivers. Perhaps he could pick up a few tips to improve his technique.

What a delight! The swim and gym centre looked splendid. It was a very modern building. It appeared almost brand new. It shone like a brilliant jewel amongst the more dull buildings. Mr Smile was impressed.

Inside, the décor was immaculate. Tiles and paint gleamed. Staff shone in bright new uniforms, though they did not have matching smiles. That didn't matter so much to Mr Smile – the place itself looked so very exciting.

Mr Smile couldn't wait to see the pool. He climbed a set of stairs and pushed open the door leading to the spectators' balcony. He stopped dead still.

Before him lay the perfect pool. It was fifty metres in length and eight lanes wide. At one end was a great tower of diving boards. It all appeared so inviting until Mr Smile realised the pool was completely empty. There was no one swimming in it...and there was not one drop of water in it! What on earth had happened? Mr Smile rushed back to the reception desk to see it he could find out.

It took some time to find the tiny scrap of paper on the noticeboard. The note was partly hidden under other bits of old news. It read:

SWIMMING POOL CLOSED DUE TO LACK OF SWIMMERS
THE POOL WILL REMAIN DRY UNTIL SOMEONE WANTS TO SWIM IN IT. WHEN THAT HAPPENS, WE WILL ADD SOME WATER
                                        - The Management

Oh dear! Perhaps everyone had given up swimming and gone to the gym instead. Mr Smile went to investigate.

The gym was luxurious, full of the latest equipment but...nobody was using it. In fact, it was covered in dust. On closer inspection, spiders seemed to be the only creatures exercising here. The cycles and training machines were covered in cobwebs.

Mr Smile left the sports centre in a hurry. He didn't want to see more of the same. As he was leaving, suddenly something came to him. Except for the reception staff, the sports centre had been deserted during his visit. Right now it was still deserted and, Mr Smile guessed, it would remain deserted. He sighed a great sigh of despair.

Around teatime he left for the woods on the edge of the town. He must gather his thoughts and write all about what he had seen during this first month in a strange new world.

Mr Smile had already decided on his first rule of happiness:

TAKE MORE EXERCISE

Chapter Seven – April

It was late April. Mr Smile had come back to the countryside for a short holiday. It was the hottest day of the year so far.

He lay on the luscious green grass, basking in the sunshine. If he was too hot, he would hide in the shadow of the oak trees – and snooze. Later, he would return to the sun for a little doze and so on …

He reclined, thinking to himself. He was so happy to be outside, especially on days like these. He wasn't alone. Everything seemed to want to escape and spend time in the great outdoors.

Soon the fledgling birds would be leaving the nest. The tadpoles would become froglets, crawling across the new lands. Butterflies would break out of their chrysalises. Bees would leave the hive. Dandelion seeds would be whisked up by the wind and transported to another world.

So, what about the town? The weather was set fair for a few days; Mr Smile would take a look.

"The park on a Sunday," Mr Smile decided.

It was daybreak when he arrived – too early for people who liked a rest after a busy week's work. No wonder the place was deserted. They would soon appear. First would be the early morning joggers, keen to get the day off to a good start. There would be the dog walkers too. For them and their pets, there was nothing quite like the smells and sounds of the breaking day. There was the peace and calm to be had before others came visiting. The dogs would have slept well and like nothing better than to chase the first stick of the day.

After breakfast, the keen children would come to the park, full of toast and energy! Football games would start up. A tennis ball would take its maiden flight as a game of catch began. Some of the parents would put down their newspapers or cease their adult chatter – and play. Swings would be swinging and seesaws would be seeing and sawing.

Later, Mr Smile guessed, the roundabout would be covered in children, turning faster and faster. There would be great games of rounders as more and more people joined in the fun. It wouldn't matter how good you were, you would be a proper part of it and so enjoy it.

There would be many games of chase on the go, all at once. Children would swarm through the woods, on to the grassy parts, on and over the climbing frames and round the circuit again.

By late afternoon, surely the park would be full to the brim with people escaping their homes to enjoy the great outdoors. The air would be charged with the sound of laughter and shouts of joy.

After tea, the little children would rest at home perhaps but the bigger ones would return to make the most of their freedom before school on Monday….

All day, Mr Smile waited and waited and waited. He saw a lone jogger, a single dog walker and his lame dog, one family…nothing more.

The sun was setting. He strolled across the park from one side to the other. He saw collapsed football posts, lying in the long grass that had not been mowed. On the tennis courts there were holes in the playing surface. There were holes in the sad and droopy nets.

The swings, slides, roundabouts and seesaws were all rusted. Mr Smile doubted if any of them would ever move again. He didn't want to try; it was all too depressing.

59

"Better leave this place," he said to himself, heading for the big black gates.

As he approached the exit, a man in a black uniform appeared with keys in hand and set about locking the gates. For a moment, Mr Smile forgot that he was invisible and that his voice could not be heard.

"Wait, wait! I have to get out! I...."

Too late! The solemn park keeper had done his job. He turned on his heel and was gone, putting the keys in his pocket.

It wasn't easy climbing the high gates with the spikes on the tops but Mr Smile managed it. He couldn't wait to leave the park behind. Turning to go, he caught sight of a notice bolted to the gates. It read:

WE TRUST THAT ALL CITIZENS WILL ENJOY USING THE PARK AND ITS FACILITIES. WE THEREFORE REQUEST THAT ALL CITIZENS ABIDE BY THE FOLLOWING RULES:
1. **NO LAUGHING. NO SHOUTING. NO SUDDEN NOISES OF ANY KIND**
2. **NO RUNNING OR FAST WALKING**
3. **RESPECT THE PLAY EQUIPMENT**
4. **ALL DOGS ON LEADS AT ALL TIMES**

Mr Smile gave up reading the rules. Instead, his attention was drawn to the bold print at the bottom of the notice:

DURING BUSY PERIODS CITIZENS MAY BE ASKED TO RESTRICT THEIR STAY IN THE PARK TO A MAXIMUM OF HALF AN HOUR. THIS IS TO ENSURE ALL CITIZENS HAVE THE OPPORTUNITY TO VISIT.
ENJOY YOURSELVES
BY ORDER – THE TOWN PARK AUTHORITY

Mr Smile headed off toward the edge of the town. He always enjoyed a walk. He had never owned a car; his legs took him everywhere. Not so for the people of this town, he thought. The pavements were empty. Weeds grew between the paving stones, some of which were broken or missing; nobody seemed keen on repairs. The roads, on the other hand, were always busy and very well looked after.

Mr Smile wasn't used to the traffic. He waited nervously at the pedestrian crossings. The green man appeared. Cars coming from both directions slammed on their brakes and came to a screeching halt. The drivers scowled, shook their heads and looked at the crossing. Only then did Mr Smile realise his mistake – yet again! "When will I stop forgetting I am invisible?"

He dashed across the road and didn't look back. He made for the main shopping street. His heart thumped. His breathing was fast.

The high street was safe from cars. Good! He could relax a little. Sunday night and the shoppers were gone. Once more, he walked alone under the bright lights.

Progress was slow. Like a moth, Mr Smile was attracted to the fascinating shop window displays. There was so much for a roving reporter to investigate. He stared and stared. All this fashion, all that electrical equipment. Beauty products to buy...medicines to make you better. Coffee to pick you up. Cakes to fill you up. Fish and meat. Fruit and vegetables. Take away food. Eat in food. Smart and elegant – all of these shops. Busy and successful – like the baker's at home.

Mr Smile could see the attraction of such places but not for himself. No, instead he was interested in the large shop at the end of the high street – "The Great Big Outdoor Store". How exciting!

Imagine the display: outdoor jackets; outdoor trousers; hats and gloves; boots and shoes; tents; sleeping bags; survival packs. Mr Smile gazed at the window in disbelief: the lights were off; the shelves were empty; the window was whitewashed. A white poster-size piece of paper occupied its centre. Written in angry red felt tip it read:

WE ARE CLOSED – FOREVER. WE WOULD LIKE TO THANK OUR CUSTOMERS FOR THEIR SUPPORT OVER THE LAST TWO YEARS BUT WE CAN'T BECAUSE WE DIDN'T HAVE ANY CUSTOMERS AND NOBODY SUPPORTED US

Mr Smile shook his head, turned and walked and kept on walking, not sure where he was going. It had been a difficult day but he had learned a lesson. The second rule of happiness:

SPEND TIME OUTDOORS

Chapter Eight – May

Early morning in early May and Mr Smile was in town, observing the children on their way to school and the parents on their journeys to work. The weather? Cloudy but dry, he noted.

As usual in this world, nobody walked unless it was the short distance to and from the car or bus. Actually, they did not walk, they stumbled. Their eyes were glazed over. They wore no expressions upon their faces. Their movements appeared automatic. Watching them, Mr Smile found it hard to stay awake.

There was little or no conversation but their mouths did move – to yawn. There was a great deal of yawning going on. It seemed as though they might swallow each other.

In the cars and on the buses, passengers – children and adults alike – slept or simply stared into space, blinking occasionally. Most drivers were completely the opposite. They were wide-eyed, twitchy and anxious to get on with it. However, this was only because they had drunk numerous cups of coffee to help themselves stay awake.

One or two drivers had, apparently, forgotten their morning drink and pulled over on to the pavement and fallen asleep. Their passengers didn't seem to notice or care.

Mr Smile followed the trail of zombie children as they staggered from their cars and buses on to the school playground. The bell sounded and they fell into school, dragged themselves down corridors and collapsed into their classroom seats.

Mr Smile sat at the back of the classroom, a puzzled look upon the only smiling face to be seen. Pupils and teacher were silent. Minutes ticked by. Slumped over his desk, the teacher sat with his head in his hands. From time to time he would blink furiously and lift his eyes to the window. All the pupils were resting or sleeping with eyes closed and heads on desks. Some were snoring.

Eventually the teacher's attention moved a very short distance to the laptop on his desk. Its bright light seemed to startle him. He spoke!

"Charlie Adams," he said quietly and without any interest. "Charlie Adams," a little louder but with no more enthusiasm. "Charlie Adams," the effort to up the volume seemed to cause great pain.

Wherever the boy was, he wasn't responding to his name – the first on the register. His classmates remained as they were, perhaps snoring a little louder to block out the unwelcome interference.

Like a spineless puppet, the teacher made one last great effort to sit up in his chair. "Charlie Adams!" he shouted in desperation before falling back into his seat.

A boy at the front of the classroom stirred, lifting his head just long enough to whisper, "Good morning, Mr Reed," before letting it fall back to his pillow of a desk.

So the routine continued, each pupil barely able to answer their name. By the end of the register, the whole class seemed to be sleeping again.

Perhaps the task of registration had woken Mr Reed, at least a little. He yawned for a full five seconds and attempted to rise to his feet. He was a little unsteady at first but he managed it.

"Class, this is simply not good enough," he announced in a near normal voice. "Let's wake up shall we and start the day."

The snoring stopped. The pupils slowly lifted their heads and then gradually forced themselves into an upright position. Their faces were miserable, of course, but it was the way they stared that Mr Smile found worrying.

"Today, as usual, we will begin with our PE class. And, as usual, we are going to make a special effort to wake up ready for our Maths and Literacy at ten o'clock. What are we going to do?"

"We are going to wake up, sir," came the robotic reply.

"Right then, line up and into the hall."

Somehow the pupils made it into the hall where they split into groups for different exercise routines. 'Exercise' however, was clearly not an accurate description of what followed.

A group of boys tried to pass a football between them. They should have trapped the ball and moved it on, quickly. Instead, they would trip over the ball and, sometimes, fall to the floor like skittles. After five minutes only three of the six were standing. The ball had escaped to the other side of the hall and no one was making an attempt to retrieve it.

Those asked to use the climbing frame were still standing, yawning, at ground level. They had made an attempt to grasp hold of the bars but had since given up and put their hands in their pockets.

The press-up and pull-up group had failed from the start and were practising lying down instead. Throwing and catching were a disaster. Running was out of the question; walking was difficult. Still, at least the air in the hall was cool and its floor cold and hard. There could be no return to sleep.

"Well, time is moving on. We'd better return to class. Put the equipment away and line up at the door." Mr Reed waited a long, long time for his struggling athletes to accomplish the task. Mr

Smile left the school as Mr Reed's class filed back to their studies.

"This is making *me* sleepy. I need a change of scenery and some fresh air," he said to himself.

Rain fell steadily from dark skies but this didn't stop Mr Smile. What did it matter if you were wet? You could soon dry yourself. Sometimes the feeling of soft rainwater on your skin was a great comfort, a great wonder.

Rain or shine, the people of this world were not in the habit of taking exercise or venturing outside. They would never know the difference between the two. Yet, it took Mr Smile only twenty minutes to find the green fields, the leafy lanes and the pond. He sat on its bank, watching the raindrops fall upon its waiting waters. The ripples came and went.

"It's like smiles and happiness," thought Mr Smile. "One smile is like a raindrop – it helps others to smile and spreads happiness. Without the rain, nothing grows. Without happiness and smiles, the world is a dead place – like *this* world. But I know, I just know I can help it come to life.

Full of new energy and enthusiasm, Mr Smile returned to the town later that evening. The sun had set. He wanted to find out how these people behaved during the hours of darkness. Why were they so tired in the morning? They didn't exercise and they seemed to be prisoners in their own homes. These two habits were enough to make anyone tired – but not that tired! There **must** be something more.

So Mr Smile walked the streets of the towns, from the rich to the poor neighbourhoods and the houses in between. It was the same wherever he went. Lights shone from every window in every house. Screens flickered.

Where curtains were left drawn back, Mr Smile saw huge television screens, filling front rooms. Families watched, entranced by the magic. If it wasn't TVs, it was computers; children and adults lost in cyberspace, fingers fidgeting on keyboards.

Midnight approached. Still, tired eyes could not turn from the flashing entertainment. They could not bring themselves to close. Mr Smile rubbed his own and yawned.

By the early hours of the morning, Mr Smile felt as though he were sleepwalking. Yet most of the lights still burned; beds were empty.

At two o'clock, Mr Smile gave up. He was too tired to continue his investigation. Anyway, he had already found out what he needed to know.

The following morning, Mr Smile overslept for the first and only time in his life. He felt tired, yes, but he also felt a little irritable. He didn't like this at all.

He decided to take the day off. Returning to the pond, he threw a pebble into the water. Like the rain, the pebble made the ripples. He felt better.

He wrote and wrote and decided on his third way to find happiness. Not surprisingly, that was:

MAKE SURE YOU HAVE ENOUGH SLEEP

Chapter Nine – June

It had been a busy three months. Investigating involved working long hours, walking long distances and spending a long time writing down what it was you found out.

Mr Smile sat on a grassy sloping bank, shaded by the oak trees above him and surrounded by the hum of insects chasing brilliant flowers. He, too, was busy trying to write down words, sentences and paragraphs in his books. However, the words would not come. It was very frustrating.

He put his pen down and sighed. This had happened before. His head was all a jumble. It needed sorting out. It needed a rest. Not a sleep. Just a little time to sit and do nothing. He must let thoughts come and go and try to concentrate on the sound of silence. He must empty his mind.

Mr Smile sat there, nice and still. He could almost feel the blood flowing through his body. He became aware of his own breathing – in and out. He was rather enjoying not having to worry about a thing. After a few minutes, he opened his eyes and sat there, remaining still and silent and staring into the space all about him.

He let his thoughts come back into his head. Now the words came and with them the sentences and the paragraphs; he knew at once what he should write. He took up his pen and filled the pages.

Mr Smile understood. It was really very simple. No one could create what they wished to create without taking a little time to be still and rest. Being busy all the time, hour after hour, day after day, would not allow anyone to think properly. If you couldn't think properly and you couldn't create what you would like to create, then you couldn't be happy.

What about Mr Reed's class? They spent the first hour of the school day sleeping or trying to wake up. They must spend some part of the day working. Would they be too busy to think? Mr Smile would find out.

It was ten o'clock in the morning. PE had finished; Literacy was about to start. By now, the class were at least sitting up in their chairs although many were yawning and rubbing their eyes.

"Time to work!" Mr Reed announced suddenly, stiff as a soldier behind his desk. At once all the class sat bolt upright, eyes wide open and mouths firmly closed.

"Write an adventure story about being lost in a forest."

The writing began immediately, at a furious pace and continued for the next hour. During that time not a single head was raised and not a single pen left the paper. Mr Reed sat perfectly still, marking books. No one made a sound.

At eleven o'clock precisely, Mr Reed announced the end of the story-writing task. "Bring your books to the front and sit down ready for Maths."

The pupils did exactly as they were instructed.

"Right, you will answer questions one to a hundred from your text books."

Mr Reed sat down and marked the Literacy books, his face never changing. His pupils answered their questions, without question. Their expressions were set in stone.

The school day progressed in the same manner, whatever the subject. Lunch was eaten as quickly as possible, with little chewing and no tasting. Pupils were forced out into the playground. Out there, children simply stood about, waiting to be let back into the building.

Midday break lasted half an hour. Pupils lined up and marched back in for more of the same.

When school finished, each child made a beeline for their own home where they curled up in the company of a computer. Their eyes and ears were concentrated on screen and speakers.

All was bright light and loud sound. There was no escaping it. There was no rest.

Mr Smile continued his investigation. This time he visited the parents at work. They, too, had no interest in stopping and thinking. An adult's day at work was the same as a child's day at school. An adult would snooze and yawn and stretch until ten o'clock and then the work would really begin in the office. Each job was a mad race to be run. At six o'clock, it was all over and the office men and women would rush home to their houses.

In the houses, the girls and boys and the mums and dads hardly spoke to each other. The family must eat its food – that was the job for the evening. This refuelling was rushed. It must not interfere with the serious business of watching TV or operating a computer.

It was June 21st, the longest day of the year. Mr Smile sat upon his grassy bank, the evening shadows lengthening.

Yet, even now, there was busy-ness all about him. Nature, it seemed, did not rest at this time of year. There was too much work to be done. Winter was different. Winter was the time to be still and quiet.

What about the humans? They, too, must have their Winter, perhaps lots of Winters, spread throughout the year.

The plants and animals must rest. The human beings must spend their little Winters being instead of doing.

'It is the rule of Nature,' thought Mr Smile, 'and it is my fourth rule of happiness.'

FIND SOME TIME JUST TO THINK AND BE

Chapter Ten – July

Mr Smile had visited Mr Reed's class and the school many times and what he saw worried him.

When busy with their lessons, some of the pupils really struggled to understand what they were supposed to be learning. They would sit there, scribbling anything upon their paper. This just made them look busy. They weren't actually achieving anything. Mr Smile knew this; he'd taken a close look at their work.

Mr Reed would mark their work and return it to them covered in crosses and decorated with sharp red lines. Nothing more. He did not attempt to explain why their work was unsatisfactory. He did not offer to help them find the right answers in Maths or to improve their writing in Literacy.

The pupils at the top of the class ignored one another and those pupils who struggled with their work. It never occurred to the clever kids to share some of their skills.

Then there was the PE. If some unlucky person fell to the ground, they would stay there, sometimes for the entire lesson. Mr Reed and those left standing would simply side step the bodies strewn across the hall floor.

The same thing would happen in the playground. From time to time, a very keen pupil would bring a ball or skipping rope to school. Rarely, very rarely, a child might try to organise a running race or a game of hopscotch.

Mr Smile couldn't bear to watch what happened next. No one was used to exercising so that children became entangled in the ropes, fell over the ball or tripped over themselves. Like skittles they went down, and stayed down, in the playground.

Of course, most of the children stood still in groups, staring into space. A few might notice the string of accidents occurring about them and turn their heads briefly. No one said anything about it. No one moved.

Perhaps most upsetting of all was the sight of those lonely children who didn't belong to the playground groups. These odd pupils sat alone on benches at the edge of the playing field. They hid, huddled in their little hiding places, propped up against walls or lost in doorways.

Their arms would be wrapped about themselves; their heads would be sunk into their chests. If you could see their eyes, they would be tight shut or staring at the ground. As usual, no one noticed them. No one came over to talk to them. No one came to comfort them.

In the town too, people struggled along on their own. Elderly people laboured under the burden of shopping bags, making slow progress from the shops to their homes. Car drivers sped past them, not giving them a second thought. It wasn't often that younger people used the pavements. However, when they did, they would pass by and ignore the elderly.

Women found it difficult to push their prams on the uneven pavements. Cars parked in their way. Babies bumped and screamed. Shopping fell from the buggies. People passed on by.

Mr Smile watched as the evening meals were cooked, served and the dishes cleared and cleaned. It was exactly the same in all the houses he visited. Parents did everything; children did nothing. It was a wonder the children could eat for themselves. They were too busy thinking about themselves to bother helping their parents.

Mr Smile retreated to the countryside. He lay gazing up at his favourite oak tree. What a magnificent specimen!

Yet the oak tree could not survive by itself. It needed the sun's light and warmth to grow. It needed the rain to fall from the clouds. It needed the minerals provided by the tiny bugs working away in the soil beneath its roots. Yes, the oak tree clearly needed a lot of help.

Everything in nature needed help if it was to grow and survive. And, in a way, everything had to help everything else. The oak tree gave a home to the nesting birds and burrowing beetles. The insects helped the flowers make their seeds, the birds spread the seed and the flowers fed the bees.

Suppose if everything in nature ignored everything else?

In the town everybody was ignoring everyone else. Helping a person in need would make that person happy. The person who did the helping would also feel happy; they would feel as though they have a part to play in life, like all the parts that make up the whole of nature.

"That's it then, without a doubt!" Mr Smile told the great oak tree. "If you want to be happy – that's rule number five."

HELP OTHERS

Chapter Eleven – August

The school holidays began at the beginning of this month. Holidays! Mr Smile imagined the excitement. First there was the planning of the holiday then the journey to the holiday destination and finally the holiday itself. What fun!

Perhaps he had been wrong about the people of this world. Holidays always brought out the hidden best in people. Smiles would appear, eyes would light up and happiness abound. Yes, agreed, he had never seen a smile or a bright eye or seen a single happy person for all the five months he had been wandering these parts but this month must be different.

Mr Smile felt a great surge of hope well up inside himself. This gave him extra energy. He planned a tour all of his own, criss-crossing the country. He wanted to find out how the people here behaved at this holiday time.

He spent many hours in libraries studying maps. Which route? Where would it take him? It was so exciting! He imagined the roads, the cities, towns and villages he would pass through – the countryside and the seaside too. It would all be new. It would all be a great discovery for him!

He thought of the people of this country planning their holidays. Some of them, perhaps quite a lot of them, would be leaving the country! Others would be travelling great distances – further than himself – to discover hidden parts of their own country.

Families would be sat together, studying maps and imagining all the little stages of their journey and what their final destination would bring them.

Of course, people always thought of what the weather might be like but there was so much more to find out.

For instance, if they were heading for the sea, would it be bluer than their own? What would it be like to swim in beautiful coves? What about the waves and the life in the water? How warm would the water be? One question would lead to another.

Mr Smile's mind swam with their enquiries. What about the people? What about the food and drink? What about the campsite, cottage, apartment or hotel? The town or the city? The countryside? The wildlife?

"Wow!" gasped Mr Smile. "It's mind boggling."

Travelling was an education, that's what it was. He thought of his own journeys and how much he had learnt. There were so many new things to see, hear, touch, taste and smell out there in holiday land.

There were even aeroplanes and boats to take you still further. He had never travelled on a boat or aeroplane but he imagined just how thrilling it would be to do so.

He must see the excitement for himself. Mr Smile would take a tour of the ports and airports of this country.

It was not at all what he had expected. Aircraft sat still on the tarmac, boats bobbed in harbours. The crowds should come but they didn't. The skies and the seas were nearly empty. Hardly anyone wanted to take off or set sail. The few who did showed not a glimmer of excitement at the prospect.

'Ah well,' said a very disappointed Mr Smile to himself. 'Perhaps it was too expensive or too much trouble to travel such a long way. Perhaps there was just as much fun to be had travelling within your own country.

'That's it, of course! I'll bet the seaside towns are full to the brim of families having fun at the beach. In the countryside there won't be a space left on which to pitch your tent. In the towns and cities, visitors will arrive and fill the hotels and boarding houses. "No vacancies" signs will appear in the windows of every Bed and Breakfast cottage.'

It wasn't to be. Beaches were covered in seawater and little else. One or two tents appeared and soon disappeared. Hotel owners shook their heads and closed the doors of their empty premises.

Mr Smile could not believe his eyes. It was worse, far worse, that he could ever have imagined. Where were all the people, then? What were they doing?

He knew the answer before investigating: they were in their homes, of course. From time to time, children might emerge to visit the shops or spend a few minutes in the park or sometimes even walk or cycle a few hundred metres. However, they soon returned to the safety of their house. Many of the parents were still working. What was the point in holidays? You may as well earn the money instead.

So the holiday month of August passed much the same as any school month. It was sad and dreary.

Still, Mr Smile had thoroughly enjoyed his travels. He had managed to make himself very, very happy through his efforts. It hadn't all been easy but it was definitely worth it.

'So,' he concluded, 'Rule six....'

PLAN A TRIP – IT DOESN'T HAVE TO BE FAR

Chapter Twelve – September

On the first day of the month, Mr Smile stood on a mountain top, one thousand metres above the sea. Far below, lay the lush green valley with its ribbon lakes and soft woodlands, its farms and cosy cottages. Up here, the world was harsh, remote and lonely.

Lonely – like the mountain – that was how he felt. Mr Smile had been away from home for six months, half a year! Home was such a long, long way away. You wouldn't see it from here, no point in straining your eyes.

Home instead must be in his head and his heart. It was all about his memories of home and how they made him feel. He could never forget his home.

'So, I'm not lonely, after all,' Mr Smile told himself, 'I have my memories to keep me company.'

His friends were his most treasured memories. How he longed to listen to their stories, to tell them his stories, to smile for them and see their smiles, to laugh and giggle together.

In this world, he was invisible. If only he could make himself seen, just for a short while. But what good would that do? These people barely seemed to speak to each other. There were certainly no smiles to be seen. Laughing and giggling was unheard of.

Anyway, right now he must work. The work would not last forever. Another three months – not long. Not like the mountain – no end in sight for the mountain.

"One fine day, people will come and visit you. Thousands of them. You wait and see what happiness can bring."

The mountain didn't answer but Mr Smile was sure his every word had been heard and understood.

Mr Smile sat down on the smooth weathered stone and gazed out across the surrounding ups and downs of the patchwork fields.

"They'll be waiting for me," Mr Smile told the attentive rocks, "I know it. We've been friends for too long. They will have been lonely too, without me. As soon as they catch sight of me, they will come running towards me, waving and shouting and...smiling! Right now though, I've a very important job to do," he announced, getting to his feet. "I bid you good day, sirs." He laughed a cheeky laugh and began his descent along the snaking gravel path.

It was the first day of the new school year. Mr Smile was back in town. He stood outside the school gates; he knew the place well by now and recognised a lot of the pupils, especially from Mr Reed's class.

As expected, the children didn't look at all happy as they climbed or fell out of the cars and buses. They were terribly sleepy, perhaps even worse than usual. In fact, they were even more miserable than usual.

Well, who would be happy to have come back to school after weeks of holiday? All this would change, thought Mr Smile, as the children stumbled into the playground and caught sight of their long-lost schoolmates.

They probably wouldn't have seen each other for four weeks and a bit. Each would have spent nearly all of that time hidden in their houses. Each must be desperate to meet up and chat.

'Perhaps, just perhaps, I may hear laughter and see smiles.' Mr Smile crossed his fingers and looked around the playground.

Good. There were groups of children standing together and the groups were larger than he had seen before. Good! There were none of those children lost alone on the edge of the crowds. Good!! The children had woken up – well, they had woken up a little. At least no one had their eyes shut and there wasn't too much yawning to be seen.

Silence. Not very good. Staring, perhaps just a blink of an eye. This was not good. Very little to talk about, it appeared. Nothing to smile and even less to laugh about. No good at all.

A quick nod of the head. Nothing more. That was supposed to say it all. A single word of a greeting, "Hello," and the same response.

The fun was over. The line of children filed into the waiting school entrance, each child a little island, separate from the others.

'What price a good friend?' Mr Smile considered. A good friend must be worth a great deal of money, more than he could possibly imagine. So, he, Mr Smile, was in fact a very rich person and that made him smile.

However, he must be careful to keep his friends if they were so valuable. They must not be neglected or forgotten. He ought to tell them just how much they meant to him.

The seventh rule of happiness:

SPEND TIME WITH YOUR FRIENDS

Chapter Thirteen – October

Mr Smile was fascinated. He tried not to stare too hard; people might think him odd.

'Oh no!' he chuckled to himself. 'I'm forgetting again. I can stand here as long as I like. No one cares about the invisible man.'

The house was very, very grand. It stood in a row of equally magnificent houses, each detached from the other. Each had its own extensive gardens, front and back. Built to last, each was a gentleman's castle – well, not quite – couples or small families lived inside.

'Enough room for ten or twenty people,' Mr Smile considered.

From the front, the houses overlooked the beautifully wooded parkland: a step or two away from paradise, or so it would seem.

Mr Smile stood there on the driveway of number ten, bathed in a beautiful pool of early morning sunshine. He gazed all around in wonder. He had climbed the great electric gates of the house; he wanted a closer look. Next to Mr Smile sat three shiny new cars.

At precisely seven o'clock, the great door of the house opened. A man, the father Mr Smile guessed, led the way to the waiting cars. A lady of about the same age, the mother, followed. Behind her came a much younger lady and two small children either side of her: a girl and boy.

The father climbed into his car, the mother into hers and the young lady and the children into the third. The gates opened. The cars left. The gates closed. No one said a word or exchanged a glance.

Mr Smile couldn't help himself; he had to find out more. He spent the next day investigating the father's movements. Mr Smile hid in the car (well, *sat* in the car – he didn't have to hide because he was invisible) and travelled to work with him.

Mr Smile watched as the man spent every minute of the day working hard in his lonely office. The father arrived home late in the evening, exhausted.

The mother did exactly the same in a different lonely office in another building in another part of the same town.

The young lady, the nanny, took the children to school. It was a very short journey that took a very long time because, as usual, the roads were clogged. During the day and the evening, the nanny cleaned the house and prepared the family meals.

The father spoke of buying another house. The family owned another already but it wasn't altogether suitable so he could be bothered to use it any more. No, what he wanted was a house in a different country with more sunshine and no rain. It would be built high up on a hillside overlooking the sea. It would be big, of course, bigger than this one. He would like the house; they would all like the house.

Mother was tired of the family house. "We need to move to another area. We need better views. I'm tired of the trees. I need mountains and lakes. I would like to move to a new place; we would all love to live in a new place."

The children were upset about the car. It wasn't new anymore. It was three months old. Other cars had comfier seats and a smoother ride, better in-car entertainment and a blacker tint to the privacy glass. They would love to upgrade the car; the whole family would love to upgrade the car.

The nanny didn't say anything. She was simply tired. All she wanted was a little peace and quiet - but nobody else did.

Father and mother were busy working to earn the money for the next move or house or car.

They were too busy to look after their children (that was what they paid the nanny to do). The children were too busy following in their parents' footsteps to think for themselves. The nanny was simply too busy.

The father and the mother told the children the truth: when they grew up, they would have to be very busy, working very hard to keep all *their* belongings. The more money you had, the more belongings you could have – and the children were growing up longing for belongings.

After a week's hard study, Mr Smile was satisfied that he understood about money and wanting more and more things. However, he was tired and needed to rest, to think about it all. What better than a couple of days' strolling around the parkland opposite? He could think of nothing more pleasant. Right now, he didn't want a bigger park or a park with more trees and a lake and fountain; it wouldn't make him feel any better than he did now. He'd soon get used to the lake and fountain and then he'd want something different and then something after that.

That was it! A person might keep on buying things or changing things, hoping that one day those things would make a big, big difference and make them happy. Instead, the belongings made them **unhappy** because they could not see the other things in life that might make them happy. Their minds were set on having more. They were slaves to their belongings. Their belongings owned them.

So, if it was happiness you were looking for, having less was actually worth more. What an odd way to think about things but, when you'd thought about it for long enough, you couldn't help thinking it was true.

Mr Smile was delighted with his stroll in the woodland. He enjoyed every second of it. However, he was tired. He was very glad he didn't have to think too much more – or at least not for the moment.

'Well, well, that's it then. One thing's for sure, trusting in money and wanting more, won't make you happy, " he said to himself. "That's the eighth way to happiness…"

DON'T TRUST MONEY
TO MAKE YOU HAPPY

Chapter Fourteen– November

Late November. Christmas was coming. In the massive shopping mall Mr Smile wandered and weaved amongst the crowds. Dazed by the bright lights, he could not believe his eyes. All about him were smiling faces belonging to people of all ages. Agreed, the smiles belonged to the advertisements in the shop windows but at least it was a start.

This must be what Christmas was all about in this world, a festival to celebrate smiling that would make everyone smile.

Mr Smile needed to know more. He swerved across a line of approaching shoppers. Inside the department store he moved up and down the floors – slowly. He had never seen so many people – and all of them crushed inside a shop. They didn't look happy about it. Not like the people in the advertisements. *Their* faces beamed like stars in a dark sky. Whatever you might choose to buy, their happy faces would persuade you it was the right thing to do.

Perfumes, handbags, shoes, suits, ties, toys, the must-haves and the latests. If you gave those gifts at Christmas, eyes would light up the darkest corners of the world.

It seemed that people believed what the advertisements told them. They were busy, very busy handing over money in exchange for the promise.

Shopping bags were big and full. Hands were full of shopping bags. Escalators, stairs and lifts were full of the heavily laden Christmas shoppers. The whole store groaned under the weight of all those presents – and everyone appeared more miserable than ever.

'Not a joyful occasion, this Christmas shopping,' thought Mr Smile to himself as he finally emerged from the scrums of the department store. He really couldn't understand how the people of this world managed to make it such an unhappy time.

Gradually his breathing and his heartbeat returned to normal.

'Still, there are the presents themselves, the celebration of giving and receiving. Perhaps Christmas will weave its magic spell after all.'

On second thoughts, Mr Smile wasn't at all convinced it would. Outside the mall and back on the streets again, people appeared just as gloomy. For those people in this world, perhaps something about Christmas had turned a little sour. He would have to investigate further.

Mr Smile sat at the back of the classroom. Mr Reed gave an order.

"As you all know, the time we call Christmas is fast approaching. Write in your own words, what this time is really about."

He bowed his head and the children began their task. They filled one or two pages. An hour later, their pens had finished moving across and down the page. It was lunchtime. The classroom emptied.

Mr Smile sifted through the pile of paper. The style of writing was very odd. Each child's ideas were more or less the same although some wrote more than others. The writing itself was very neat, the letters properly upright and the words very close together on the page. He picked up one piece of work and read it very carefully – after all, he had a particular interest in poetry.

What Christmas is all about

Christmas is a time
To get what you want
You want a lot of things
You get a lot of things

Tell your parents
What you want
Tell them lots of things
You get lots of things

Each year I get a lot of things
I want a lot of things

I don't want any old things
I want lots more new things.

He picked up another.

Christmas
Is getting
And wanting
More and new.

And another...

Come to the shops
Have a good look round
Really have a good look
In all the best places in the shops
Start buying presents for me in September
Take loads of money with you
Make the presents really big and expensive
And don't buy me old things
Still keep buying me more and more new things.

By Danny Thompson 6R

Mr Smile wasn't impressed! The writing had no feeling in it – but there again it did, only it was so simple and clumsy. Yes, the writing said a lot to Mr Smile. It left him in no doubt as to how these children felt about Christmas. What about everyone else in this world? They probably felt the same.

Mr Smile re-read the poems. Yes, that was it! He suddenly realised. All the time he had been here, he had never heard the words 'thank you'. If you were never grateful for something – anything – then how could you be happy when you received it?

Mr Smile imagined all the parents across this land, busy shopping, wrapping the presents and hiding them away ready for the great day. They would give the presents on that day but it wouldn't bring them any pleasure. They knew that their children would not thank them for the gifts. The children would want more and more. They would never, for one moment, be satisfied.

Mr Smile thought about all the gifts he'd been given...

'Now let me see. Ah yes, first of all there's being alive – that's the biggest gift. Then there's food and water and somewhere to sleep. Friends and Nature. Good days...and bad days! Thinking. Pens and paper. Running and standing still. Sleeping under the stars and waking to catch the rising sun. Being useful... there are quite a few to start with but the list goes on and on and on.

'Yes, Christmas or not, it would be a good idea to say thank you every day or every hour or every minute or second: whenever you felt like it, I suppose. Right now, I'm very thankful to have found out my ninth way to happiness...'

SAY 'THANK YOU'

Chapter Fifteen – December

Friday December 1st

A steady drizzle fell from the early evening sky. The weather did not deter the crowds of people who filled the main shopping street. Indeed, this was a special event – it was the only day of the year the street was closed to traffic.

A stage had been erected and on it stood the town's mayor. He rambled on and on and on and his voice was terribly dull but that didn't seem to bother the spectators. That is to say, they didn't leave. However, they didn't look particularly interested either. They simply stared at the man, much as the pupils stared at Mr Reed.

The moment finally came when the mayor stopped talking. A woman appeared on the stage, the star guest for the evening. Apparently, she was a real celebrity, a singer well-known to millions of television viewers. They had voted for her and now she had a new job – being famous. The mayor persuaded her to sing a song. She sang it. The people looked at her in the same way they looked at the mayor. Nobody clapped.

Amongst the crowd, Mr Smile waited for the real highlight of the evening. He had never seen anything like it before. Just how magical would it look? He watched the celebrity finger reach for the switch and …

The Christmas lights came on! All along the street, up and down the buildings, they pierced the gloom of the night.

"What a wonderful show!" exclaimed Mr Smile.

The crowd didn't seem to think so. Or did they? It was very hard to tell. There was not a hint of a smile, just as Mr Smile expected.

"Who can switch these people on?" Mr Smile asked himself. "Me, I hope!" he replied. "I hope I have the magic; I think I do."

Mr Smile decided he would work all day in the library and sleep in there at night. Outside it was freezing cold. It was cold enough to snow. Newspapers were forecasting a white Christmas but the people ignored the headlines. Snow was a dream belonging to ages past.

It was a shame. Snow would have brightened up this world. Children might have run outside and built snowmen and etched smiles upon their faces.

This world was too miserable and grey for snow. The snowflakes probably took one look at it and decided not to fall. In truth, it was actually too cold to snow and, for days, a grey blanket of impenetrable gloom had hung over the town. Oh for a beautiful pure white blanket of snow, reflecting the light from the sky and waking up the world! It would fill folk with a newfound energy.

Instead, the dull days and dark nights sapped their strength. The town's people moved in slow motion; faces were set in stone. Only the Christmas lights broke through the tight dark seal but it was all too little for tired people.

Of course, Mr Smile was saddened by their attitude. Still, he dared to hope for better. He must never give up but must work his very hardest under the bright, bright lights of the library.

So, on the morning of December 4th at precisely nine o'clock, Mr Smile stepped through the library's opening doors. He found the perfect table, tucked away in a quiet corner where no one could bother him or, more likely, not see him and sit on him.

Comfortable in his writer's chair, he undid the straps of the rucksack and lifted two of the notebooks from within. Ceremoniously, he placed them upon the table in front of him. He breathed deeply. His fingers began to flick through the pages. Now, what exactly was it he had been writing all this time?

He had been very, very busy – no doubt about that. There were no white spaces left on the pages. Even the margins had filled with notes, important notes scribbled in tiny handwriting. The covers of the books were a little battered and pages turned over at the edges. Grass stains, mud spots and watermarks were a constant feature of the volumes.

How could he have written all these words? He had never written more than a few letters in his life and, he remembered, the odd very short story, but nothing like this. This work was inspired. It was amazing how passion could make a person achieve more than they ever thought possible.

Mr Smile closed the books and set himself to rest and have a good think. He slept a while but that didn't matter. Libraries often made you sleepy. If he did snore, no one would have heard him.

The sleep clearly did him a lot of good. Bursting with energy and confidence, he went about putting the notes into order. He decorated pages with arrows, asterisks and underlining. His sure and brave hand took to crossing out words, sentences, paragraphs and sometimes nearly a whole page. He juggled what was left.

It was exhausting. He stood up and walked several times around the library. Then he began to shuffle his words to make proper sentences. He took those words and lined them up like soldiers in formation. He was happy with the sentences now.

They made sense. Each word was in the right place. He went on to join those sentences to make new paragraphs, pages and chapters.

This new book was very nearly complete. He was happy – for now. Later he would check his work again and again, if necessary. This was what Mr Reed would call 'good editing' but it was something he and all of his class, including Danny Thompson, never ever bothered with. By editing or improving his work, Mr Smile managed to squeeze two notebooks of notes into one – but that was not all.

Mr Smile was still desperately searching for his tenth way to happiness; nine just didn't sound right. It was one short of ten, which was a lovely even, round number.

Now, he wasn't even thinking about it when suddenly the answer came to him. He was sitting there, staring in to space when he realised the answer was right there, staring him in the face. Yes – it was actually written all over his face and he would have found it earlier if he had taken a good look in the mirror.

Smiling: The final piece of the happiness jigsaw! Smiling, in itself, made you feel happy. It was at moments like this that he wanted to tell the whole world – but he would have to wait a little while longer. Still, he couldn't help himself. He leapt from his seat.

"Pass it on!" shouted Mr Smile. "The tenth way to happiness..."

SMILING

Chapter Sixteen - Christmas

There! Now he felt even better. He sat back down and composed himself. He must begin again. His next task was to make two **best** copies of his book.

As he was the patient kind, he enjoyed this sort of work. He loved to take the scruffy-looking words from his notes and change their appearance completely. He delighted in the straight, straight lines and the curves and loops of the letters. The gaps between words were just so, the full stops – smart dots dropped into exactly the right position.

In this way, Mr Smile made the books he was so proud of. The content was divided into ten chapters. Each chapter explained one of the ten ways to happiness. The author told how his investigations over the last ten months had led him to find each of the secrets.

With one day of his library stay remaining, Mr Smile added the last full stop to the last sentence of the last chapter.

"There!" he exclaimed in triumph. "I've done it; I've finished!"

He closed the two books and jigged a Mr Smile jig all around the library, several times. Breathing heavily, he collapsed in his seat, closed his eyes and waited for closing time.

Come opening time the next day, he began work on his final creation in the book. This was the title page. It had to look good. He wanted it perfect. The writing should be very neat, of course, but also very big and bold. How about illustrations? "Just one," he thought.

Now, most important of all, what about the title itself? It came to him straight away – 'Ten Ways to Happiness' – simple, nice and short.

So Mr Smile crafted this page. It took him several hours. He dare not make a mistake. One final decision, should he add the words 'by Mr Smile'? In the end, he did. He couldn't help himself, he was so proud of his achievement. One final, final job...he signed one of the two copies.

At tea-time on the evening of December 18th, Mr Smile stepped out through the library doors. He would not return.

Out on the street it was still freezing but that didn't matter to Mr Smile. He had his plan. It made him tingle with excitement. Inside, he glowed. For once in this world, he did not notice the misery all about him. As he walked towards the house, he felt as if he were in his own little world.

He stood waiting on the pavement. He knew the mother would arrive home from work at around six o'clock. Sure enough, the car rolled up at just before six and the tired woman dragged herself from it, through the front door and into the house. Mr Smile followed right behind her.

Once inside, it was easy. Downstairs, the boy was watching a wall-to-wall TV. Its voice boomed through the lonely building. Father wasn't yet home. He was working late, as usual. Mother would be busy making the evening meal that no one would thank her for.

Mr Smile pushed open the bedroom door. It clattered against a huge speaker that stood behind it. The dim bedroom light had been left on. Other smaller lights, green and red, twinkled and glowed from all four sides of the room. TVs and computers of various sizes sat waiting on a bench that ran all around the room. An army of speakers decorated the floor underneath the bench. Several pairs of headphones lay abandoned by the bedside. The bed itself stood in the middle of the room, an island in a sea of electronics.

There wasn't much carpet to see. It was grey. The walls and the ceiling were a little bit darker grey. The duvet and pillows were black to match the curtains. There were no books in the room. There were no clothes in the room.

Mr Smile reached inside his rucksack and took out the bright red notebook. Carefully, he placed it on the pillow. He didn't want to stay here a moment longer. He turned, ran down the staircase and across the hallway. He let himself out of the front door, picked up his feet, ran again and did not stop running until he had reached the woods.

He made his bed in a little cave, hollowed out from the rock that lay beneath an umbrella of oak branches. Mr Smile curled up in a ball and wrapped his blankets about him. Here, away from the misery, the hope inside him burnt like a fire. It kept him warm all night long.

The very next morning, he ran, ran like the wind, all the way back into town. Just after nine o'clock, he walked into the school. Hiding in the store-room, he waited, listening out for Mr Reed's class to come slipping and slopping down the corridor on their way to the hall. The sleepy parade passed by and slept-walked on for their PE lesson.

Mr Smile crept down the corridor too and took up his spying position. If he stood on tiptoe, he could stretch to see through the glass window in the top half of the door. However, he must be ready to duck down at any moment. For the first time in a long while, someone might see him. Carefully, he watched.

This morning the class behaved as normal. All of them were clumsy and useless in their attempts to exercise...except for one strange, strange boy.

He was the only pupil running about and climbing and kicking and throwing balls and leaping and dancing around, treading over the sleeping bodies of his classmates.

Mr Reed rubbed his eyes in astonishment or rather, he rubbed his eyes and looked a tiny bit surprised. The boy seemed mad; he had too much life in him. All this energy made Mr Reed feel dizzy; he had to sit down.

Mr Smile saw the boy's eyes. Were they really grey or was there a hint of blue? There was! The more excited the boy became, the wider his eyes and the bluer their colour.

Mr Smile could not wait any longer. He had to know. He thought he knew but he needed proof. He couldn't go on hiding. He pushed the door open and stood just inside the hall.

All at once, Danny Thompson stopped dead in his tracks. His jaw dropped, his eyes were wider than ever and fixed upon Mr Smile. Seconds passed; he remained frozen. Then, it happened! Gradually a smile appeared on his face and finally he found his missing voice.

"Mr Smile!" he cried and again, "Mr Smile!"

Without hesitating he ran across the hall and flung his arms around his hero. Mr Smile was nearly crushed breathless by the passion of Danny's embrace.

He must try to make Danny listen.

"Danny, I'm so, so pleased to meet you after such a long time but we must talk later, not now. Meet me on the playing field at break-time.

Please," he hurried on, "I must go now. See you later. Watch out Danny, Mr Reed's on his way!"

Mr Smile was gone.

Danny Thompson stood there bubbling with happiness and excitement. It was too much for Mr Reed. He'd been sitting quite comfortably. Now he had to struggle to his feet and wander over to the other side of the hall. What to do with the boy? Never in all his thirty years of teaching, had he witnessed such extraordinary behaviour. The child was hallucinating. The child was excited. The child was not his usual miserable self.

"Christmas," Mr Reed muttered to himself. "Christmas is the cause. He's getting carried away with the thought of all those presents. He must be a very sensitive child."

He would have to be careful with the boy.

"Danny, are you feeling quite well this morning? Only I've noticed you are a little busy and your face, well, it's...it's changed a bit." Mr Reed was struggling with his words. He wasn't at his best this time of the morning.

Suddenly the smile disappeared from Danny's face. The energy drained from his body and he stood there looking limp and miserable.

Mr Reed was relieved. "That's better, Danny."

"I know sir, I don't know what happened, sir. Maybe," Danny had to think quickly, "maybe it was something in my cereal this morning sir. Maybe it was some of those additives, sir."

"Yes, yes, quite," Mr Reed agreed.

"I'm back to normal now though." Danny faked a yawn.

"Are you sure?"

"Yes sir, really sir." Danny yawned again and let his limbs wilt a little more. "I think I need to lie down now sir, if you don't mind."

Mr Reed looked about the hall. There were several other pupils flat out on the floor.

"Of course, Danny. Have a good long rest – as long as you like."

Danny spent the rest of the PE lesson flat on his back. It wasn't easy. He really wanted to leap up and dance around the hall, celebrating. That would come later, he decided with a secret grin on his hidden face.

Literacy. Danny looked well again. At least, that's what Mr Reed thought as he settled into his chair. The boy was busy writing. He had that serious sad look about him. Good. No more nonsense.

However, Danny was hiding something from his teacher. Danny was busy writing what he wanted to write, not what Mr Reed had asked for. Danny had to try desperately hard not be excited with his work; he didn't want Mr Reed asking any more questions.

When he had finished his secret writing, Danny quickly wrote another piece. It was all about Winter, Mr Reed's idea. Danny made sure this writing was dull – all about keeping warm and staying inside with the central heating on. Mr Reed would love that.

Danny dropped his 'Winter' work on the class pile. He left the classroom with the secret paper folded safely in his deep pocket.

Out on the playground, Danny left the rest of his class standing about in odd groups, looking lost. He wandered off to the edge of the playing field with his head down, trying to appear utterly fed up.

Nearing the edge of the playing field, he looked up and saw Mr Smile. Danny couldn't help himself. He tried walking quickly but the excitement was too great – Danny burst into a run. Danny didn't care now. Anyway, no one would be watching. He screeched to a halt before Mr Smile. Now Danny wore a smile of his own.

"I read the book! I'm going to tell everyone! It's so easy, we can all be smiling – the whole world. You're just so brilliant, Mr Smile! I dreamed of you and now my dream's come true. I wrote a poem for you just now, in Literacy. Mr

Reed doesn't know. I can't let him know now. Not yet. They'll think I am mad if they see me happy. I'll have to explain to them then they'll understand. You can help me too. We'll make a great team – only you'll be the leader. You're the best!"

Danny stopped for a second to draw breath. Mr Smile took his chance. "Danny, please slow down. I understand a little bit of what you're saying but the rest is a complete mystery." Mr Smile paused. "Danny, we have to make a plan together. Let's start at the beginning...

"When I left the book on your pillow last night, I didn't know if you would pick it up and read it. So, how much did you read?"

"All of it! Every word – I just couldn't stop."

"That's wonderful for you Danny. But what about the rest of them? So tell me, how are we going to help the whole world to smile? We can't have everyone reading my book."

Danny had the answer.

"We don't need everyone to read the book – just some people, a few people. I'll lend it to them and make sure they don't damage it. Those people can pass on the message to other people. Soon there'll be lots more people talking about the ten ways to happiness."

Danny stopped suddenly and spoke very seriously. "Mr Smile, we've been so miserable for so long! It's horrible to feel like that all the time. Everyone felt so sad, they just gave up. There was really nothing to live for. Nothing nice ever happened.

"Then I dreamed a dream where I asked you to come and save us. When I woke up I was happy for a second – then I was sad again. I thought it would never come true. When it did come true and I read the book last night, it was the most amazing feeling in the universe. When you feel like I do right now, you just want to tell everyone the secrets of happiness. You want them to feel happy too. Oh Mr Smile, it's just brilliant! Brilliant, brilliant, brilliant!"

Danny shouted the last word. He didn't care. No one would listen to him anyway. Not yet. Soon they would.

"It certainly is brilliant, Danny. Let me tell you, I dreamed that dream, too. That's why I came here – to help your world. You were so real in that dream, Danny. I dared to hope I might find you - and I did! But listen, Danny, I have to go back to my world. I can't stay here forever."

"You can't?"

"No."

"Not just for a while?"

"No, Danny, I have to leave today. My job is done."

"Is your world a long way away, then?"

"Yes, yes it is. So far away that it is, in fact, a completely different world."

For just a moment or two, Danny took his eyes off Mr Smile and stared at the ground. It was a terrible blow, losing Mr Smile. But, do you know what? With the smile and the happy feeling bubbling up inside of him, he, Danny Thompson, could do it!

"OK, so you have to leave...but I can do it! I can start to tell the secrets to happiness. I know I can. When you feel like I do, Mr Smile, you can do anything."

Danny dipped a hand into his pocket and pulled out the folded paper.

"Here, this poem sort of tells the story. It's about you rescuing people. I'm the kid in the poem. You tell me to pass the message on and I do. Here, have a read."

When Smile walked into Town

It was early in the morning
When Smile walked into town
Folks, they couldn't help themselves
They put their worries down.

This here face is loaded
Says Smile with a grin
You people gotta help yourselves
And learn to smile again.

But Sir, we don't know how to
Says one cute little kid
Ain't no one ever smiled round here
In all the time I lived.

Ah son, you gonna make me sad
But no, I'm Mister Smile!
Now take a good long look at me
Yeah concentrate a while.

Why sure, I feel better
Said the cute kid with a grin
Say Mister I sure feel good
Now I can smile again.

Well, Son, you take that face of yours
That's shining like the sun
You pass that smile on to folks
We've only just begun...

...Why sure the town is happy
Folks stop you on the street
Shake your hand and tell you
Isn't life just great!

Although we have our sadness
We've riches in our life
And best of all, oh yes siree!
We folks have learned to smile.

Mr Smile's eyes were wet with happy tears.

"That really is a wonderful poem! Such a happy story!"

"And it's true, thanks to you, Mr Smile! Please, please keep my poem. It's a present from me to you. You gave me the big book and I want to give you this little poem."

126

"Of course I'll keep it. I'll treasure it. Here, I'll hide it safely in my notebook." Mr Smile reached into his rucksack and pulled out the second copy of 'Ten Ways to Happiness'.

Danny was puzzled. "You have another copy of your book?"

"Yes, just the one."

"Is it for you?"

"Well, yes I suppose it is – but I do want to show it to lots of other people, people in my world. You see, Danny, the people where I come from are always smiling and happy." Mr Smile stopped to think. "Now I realise why – they are always following the rules!"

"What rules?"

"The ten ways to happiness."

"So, why do you need to show them your book?"

"Well, first of all to let them know they are doing the right thing and secondly to help them if they ever stop doing the right thing."

"I'm really excited, Mr Smile! You mean if a person keeps on doing the things to do with the ten ways to happiness, they they'll always feel happy?"

"Exactly."

"Like I feel now?"

"Yes, why not?"

"That is amazing!" Danny was thinking. "You know, I'm not afraid of anything when I'm like this. I've always been afraid, all my life. It creeps up on me. It stops me doing things. It makes me want to hide away from everyone – and everything." Danny paused. "I suppose being afraid makes me even more unhappy."

"Yes, I know what you mean," nodded Mr Smile, remembering his swim across the river.

Danny's eyes lit up. "That's it! The happiness makes the fear go away so the far can't make you unhappy."

"That's happiness for you," Mr Smile agreed. "And, as long as you are spreading happiness wherever you go, you will enjoy a wonderful life. Everything else follows, Danny. Nothing else matters as much as true happiness."

"Wow, Mr Smile, you've said it all! Do you know what? I'm going straight into the hall where they all have their lunch and I'm going to tell them everything! Then all the kids will tell each other and the whole school will be happy by home time." Danny paused. "And anyway, I *have* to do it today – it's the last day of term. Our school has to have the best Christmas ever. Then, after school, I'll go and show your book to my parents and they'll phone all their friends and soon we'll have thousands of happy adults. Tomorrow I'll go

128

to the park in the morning and to the shops in the afternoon and if everyone tells everyone else, the whole town will be happy by tomorrow night."

Danny's grin was becoming a match for Mr Smile's. Well, not quite!

"Well," said Mr Smile, "you certainly have it all worked out and I know I can trust you to spread the word. And now I know, I feel happy to be leaving."

"Do you have to go right now?"

"Yes, I do. The time is right, Danny."

Mr Smile held out a hand. Danny shook it, hard, as hard as he could.

Mr Smile's voice was just a little bit shaky. "Good bye and good luck, Danny."

Danny's voice was shaky too. "Good bye and good luck, Mr Smile."

Mr Smile turned and walked towards the school gates. He was still invisible to the pupils in the playground.

Now was a good time to escape. With Danny at work, everyone would see him and start to ask questions. He didn't want all that. He'd rather slip away all alone.

The forests and the mountains called to him. Soon he would be able to bring Arthur the good news he had always wanted to hear: where there was happiness, there was hope.

Later that afternoon, on the edge of the forest, he felt it: cold and sticky on his face. First one then another then another: snowflakes danced down from the skies above. It was going to be a white Christmas, after all.

Inspiration for Mr Smile's Investigation

Mr Smile came into being a few years ago when I wrote the poem "When Smile walked into Town". Children loved the character of Mr Smile and the sentiment contained within the verse. Helen drew him and I was an instant fan. Since then, I have used the example of Mr Smile in poetry, drama and story writing to help school children (and staff!) to find ways to be happier.

Imagine my surprise when I came across a scientifically backed article that actually listed and proved most of the techniques I had already been promoting! Suddenly the idea came to me to write a book where Mr Smile first discovers these "Ten Ways to Happiness".

Here is the original list from the article. You will see that they are portrayed *slightly* differently in the book so that younger readers can relate to them. Note too that smiling is on the list! Mr Smile is very proud of his.

David Mason 2014

1. Exercise more – 7 minutes might be enough

2. Sleep more – you'll be less sensitive to negative emotions

3. Move closer to work – a short commute is worth more than a big house

4. Spend time with friends and family – don't regret it on your deathbed

5. Go outside – happiness is maximized at 13.9°C

6. Help others – 100 hours a year is the magical number

7. Practice smiling – it can alleviate pain

8. Plan a trip – but don't take one

9. Meditate – rewire your brain for happiness

10. Practice gratitude – increase both happiness and life satisfaction

Quick last fact: Getting older will make you happier

If you want to read the original article, here is the link to paste into your browser:
http://www.collective-evolution.com/2014/01/10/10-simple-things-you-can-do-today-that-will-make-you-happier-backed-by-science/